visit us at www.abdopublishing.com

Reinforced library bound edition published in 2012 by Spotlight, a division of the ABDO Group, 8000 West 78th Street, Edina, Minnesota 55439. Spotlight produces high-quality reinforced library bound editions for schools and libraries. Published by agreement with Warner Bros.—A Time Warner Company. The stories, characters, and incidents mentioned are entirely fictional. All rights reserved. Used under authorization.

Printed in the United States of America, Melrose Park, Illinois.
052011
092011
♻ This book contains at least 10% recycled materials.

Library of Congress Cataloging-in-Publication Data

Rozum, John.
  Scooby-Doo and the monster of a thousand faces! / writer, John Rozum ; penciller, Robert Pope. -- Reinforced library bound ed.
    p. cm. -- (Scooby-Doo graphic novels)
  ISBN 978-1-59961-916-3
  1. Graphic novels. I. Scooby-Doo (Television program) II. Title. III. Title: Monster of a thousand faces!
  PZ7.7.R69Sb 2011
  741.5'973--dc22

                          2011001364

All Spotlight books are reinforced library bindings and manufactured in the United States of America.

SCOOBY-DOO!

Table of Contents

"THAT SURE WAS NICE OF TOM BURDEN TO INVITE US TO THE SET OF HIS NEW TELEVISION SERIES."

HANNA-BARBERA STUDIOS

DOES ANYONE KNOW WHAT HIS SERIES IS ABOUT?

HE SAID IT WAS SOMETHING THAT WE COULD RELATE TO, AN ANTHOLOGY SERIES WITH A DIFFERENT MONSTER FEATURED EVERY WEEK.

LIKE, AS LONG AS THE MONSTERS ARE ON MY TV AND NOT IN MY FACE, I'M ALL FOR IT.

THIS IS IT, SOUND STAGE NUMBER SIX.

IT SURE IS DARK IN HERE.

WHERE IS EVERYBODY?

MAYBE THEY'RE AT LUNCH. WHY DON'T SCOOBY AND I GO CHECK OUT THE STUDIO COMMISSARY?

DON'T BOTHER. YOU WON'T FIND *ANYONE* THERE.

NOT FROM MY SHOW, ANYWAY. OH, I DIDN'T REALIZE THAT BECOMING A PRODUCER AND DIRECTOR MEANT HAVING *TWICE* THE HEADACHES.

WHAT HAPPENED? *WHERE* IS EVERYONE?

YOU'RE PROBABLY THE ONLY FOUR PEOPLE AND A DOG WHO WOULD BELIEVE ME WHEN I SAID THAT A MONSTER SCARED THEM AWAY FROM THE SET.

ONE OF YOURS?

I *WISH.*

IF THE MONSTERS DESIGNED FOR THE SHOW WERE ANYTHING LIKE THE ONE THAT SCARED EVERYONE OFF, I'D HAVE A HIT TV SERIES ON MY HANDS.

INSTEAD I HAVE AN EMPTY SOUND STAGE AND A CAST AND CREW WHO REFUSE TO RETURN UNTIL THAT MONSTER'S TAKEN CARE OF.

DON'T YOU WORRY, MR. BURDEN. WE'LL GET TO THE BOTTOM OF THIS MYSTERY AND HAVE YOUR SHOW UP AND RUNNING IN *NO* TIME.

I HOPE SO. YOU WOULDN'T BELIEVE HOW MUCH MONEY I'M SPENDING JUST TO SIT HERE IN THE DARK, WORRYING.

LET'S SPLIT UP. DAPHNE AND I WILL LOOK FOR LEADS WITH THE CAST AND CREW MEMBERS.

YOU THREE CHECK THE STUDIO GROUNDS FOR CLUES. WHY DON'T YOU START WITH...

"...THE PROP DEPARTMENT."

RWOW!

I'LL SAY. LIKE, CHECK IT OUT, THIS PLACE IS STUFFED TO THE RAFTERS WITH ALL SORTS OF GROOVY STUFF FROM *HANNA-BARBERA* MOVIES.

LOOK, THERE'S TOUCHÉ TURTLE'S SWORD, LIPPY THE LION'S HAT, AND SOME SOME MASKS FROM THAT SHOW ABOUT THE TEENAGERS WHO SOLVED MYSTERIES WITH THAT TALKING DUNE BUGGY, AND MORE MASKS FROM THAT SHOW ABOUT THE TEENAGERS WHO SOLVED MYSTERIES WITH THAT REVOLUTIONARY WAR GHOST.

Panel 1:

ENOUGH REMINISCING, YOU TWO. WE'RE HERE TO SEARCH FOR CLUES, NOT DEMONSTRATE WHAT BIG FANBOYS YOU ARE.

LIKE, I DON'T THINK WE'RE GOING TO FIND WHAT WE'RE LOOKING FOR HERE.

Panel 2:

AS NEAT AS THESE CLASSIC MONSTER COSTUMES ARE, I DON'T THINK *ANY* OF THEM HAVE THAT REALISTIC IMPACT THAT COULD SCARE OFF TOM BURDEN'S ENTIRE CAST AND CREW LIKE HE DESCRIBED.

THESE MONSTERS HAVE MORE *CHARM* THAN *HARM*.

Panel 3:

YOU'RE PROBABLY RIGHT.

I JUST HOPE FRED AND DAPHNE ARE HAVING BETTER LUCK THAN WE ARE.

Panel 4:

THE BRILLIANT TEAM WHO CREATES ALL OF THE SHOW'S MONSTERS ARE RIGHT IN THAT ROOM.

CREATURE SHOP

THANKS FOR YOUR HELP.

Panel 5:

CAN WE HELP YOU?

I'M SORRY, THERE MUST BE SOME MISTAKE.

WE WERE TOLD THIS WAS THE ROOM WHERE ALL THE MONSTERS FOR TOM BURDEN'S TV SERIES WERE MADE.

EXIT

THAT'S RIGHT.

Panel 6:

BUT WHERE ARE ALL THE *MASKS,* AND *MOLDS,* AND *LIQUID LATEX RUBBER?*

DUDE, WHERE HAVE YOU BEEN? *NOBODY* MAKES MONSTERS THAT WAY ANYMORE. WE DO IT *ALL* ON COMPUTERS *NOW.*

THE
END!

VELMA'S MONSTERS OF THE WORLD LA VELUE

AS YOU MIGHT HAVE *GUESSED* BY THE *NAME* OF THIS EPISODE'S MONSTER, WE'RE GOING TO *FRANCE*.

JOHN ROZUM - WRITER
FABIO LAGUNA - ARTIST
SWANDS - LETTERER
HEROIC AGE - COLORS
HARVEY RICHARDS - EDITOR

"ACCORDING TO *LEGEND*, THE DEADLY LA VELUE WAS *REJECTED* FOR PASSAGE ABOARD *NOAH'S ARK* BUT FOUND A WAY TO *SURVIVE* BY DESCENDING INTO A *CAVE* NEAR WHAT IS NOW CALLED THE HUISINE RIVER IN FRANCE.

"WHEN IT *EMERGED* FROM ITS CAVE AGES LATER, IT *TERRORIZED* THE COUNTRYSIDE, *BURNING* DOWN CROPS WITH ITS SCORCHING *BREATH*, DEVOURING PEOPLE AND LIVESTOCK, AND *DESTROYING* PROPERTY.

"LA VELUE, ALSO KNOWN AS THE *PELUDA*, MEANS *SHAGGY BEAST*, A NAME GIVEN TO IT BECAUSE OF WHAT APPEARS TO BE COARSE *HAIR* COVERING ITS BODY.

"THIS HAIR WAS *ACTUALLY* THOUSANDS AND THOUSANDS OF *TENTACLES* TIPPED WITH POISONOUS *STINGERS*, WHICH IT USED TO KILL ANYONE WHO TRIED TO ATTACK IT.

"OTHER TIMES, IT WOULD *EVADE* ITS *ATTACKERS* BY WADING INTO THE *RIVER*, CAUSING TREMENDOUS *FLOODS* TO WASH OVER THE LAND.

"LA VELUE'S UNDOING FINALLY CAME WHEN IT PICKED THE *WRONG* PERSON TO EAT, A YOUNG *WOMAN* ABOUT TO BE MARRIED.

"THE WOMAN'S FIANCÉ WAS *SO* DISTRAUGHT THAT HE *TRACKED* THE MONSTER DOWN AND *CHOPPED* OFF ITS TAIL."

IT TURNED OUT THAT LA VELUE'S *ONLY* WEAKNESS WAS ITS TAIL. AS SOON AS IT WAS CUT OFF, LA VELUE DROPPED *DEAD*.

THANK GOODNESS, BECAUSE THE ONE *SHAGGY* BEAST *I KNOW* IS MORE THAN *ENOUGH* FOR ME.

THE END!